WATERS OF PASSION

Kathleen Adele
Cunningham

ISBN: 979-8-89075-714-2

4

Contents

Chapter 1 – Celebrating Success

Times Square, New York.

A group of men sat around a circular coffee table in Gregorys Coffee, awaiting their limo. Bright rays of sunshine streamed through the French windows as Lance leaned back in his chair and indicated to the waitress that he wanted another cup of coffee.

The other three men looked at him with exasperation. Henry waved his hand emphatically, "We have other *plans*. Let's not get high on caffeine already."

"That's your last cuppa for the day," said Alex, imitating a strong British accent.

All four were American to the core, but Steven, the office boy at their publishing firm, *Publishers Inc.,* was often the butt of their jokes.

Lance, Alex, Henry, and Theodore laughed heartily before Lance commented, "We've done a good job, boys! With the success of this project, our team gets a one up… All we need now is to raise the bar for the other teams by over-achieving targets this year. But now is not the time to discuss business. It's time to party!!!"

As a side business, Lance was also a motivational speaker, and that shone through in his ability to keep his team really pumped and energized. They were ever ready to achieve greater heights.

As an incentive for their commendable performance, Lance's team was off on a company-afforded luxury cruise. The anticipation and excitement in the air only increased as the time for them to start their much-awaited trip drew near.

Suddenly, Lance's phone buzzed, and before receiving the call, he looked at the others, excusing himself by explaining it was his daughter on the line.

"Hi, Angela! I'm almost ready to head towards the cruise. How are things with you?"

"Just called to wish you a safe and exciting trip, Dad. Bill will receive you at the dock when you get back," she said, referencing her husband. "I'll leave you to enjoy the cruise. Take care!"

Lance thanked Angela for the call, smiled to himself, and thought about his children. How well they had turned out despite his wife's death when they were young!

His son, Fredrik, was the elder of the two and worked as an engineer at a construction company, while Angela was a doctor at the Central Hospital. Lance never remarried, choosing instead to raise his children under his own dedicated care, which had taken up most of his time over the years, keeping him too busy to think of anything (read: anyone) else. Now that his children were grown up and busy with their own lives, Lance often felt lonely but never entertained thoughts of romance.

Lance was a well-to-do executive and loved his job at Publishers Inc. The company had given his career a solid foundation as he grew with the publishing firm and made it from one position to the next. He afforded a lavish lifestyle, and his persona reflected aristocracy. From the way he carried himself to his sense of style, everything about him boasted not only his affordability but also his good taste. Despite being a big shot, he was a man of ethics and courtesy. Never would he speak an ill word, nor did he have a temper. He was one of the most easygoing fellows in spite of his stature and always emanated a light-hearted aura that served to cheer all those around him.

He headed back to the table, where his colleagues were busy discussing their itinerary. Their adventure will take them from New York (Manhattan) through to Newport, Portland (Maine), Bar Harbor, Saint John (New Brunswick), Halifax, and back to Manhattan. A seven-night cruise to Canada and New England!

Lance joined the discussion and joked, "Nothing life-threatening, I suppose, but I hope we make it back. I don't want to leave my son-in-law stranded at the dock! He'll be there to receive me. It's too early to discuss, but anyone needing a ride will be welcome."

Theodore smiled weakly at Lance's lame joke while the others put up a laugh for their leader's benefit.

Lance got the hint and smiled in an attempt to cover up the lack of humor in his joke but patted Henry on the back, "You laugh well, young man. I take it that at least you have a sense of humor, even if I don't. My joke got through to you while Theodore was too slow on the uptake."

Lance looked around for the waitress. The longer they had to wait, the more coffee he shall have. However, Alex raised his arm and lowered Lance's hand, which he had raised to call over the waitress. "I'm telling you, Lance. Coffee and booze don't sit well together, and we're really going to party hard tonight."

"The cruise will be quite a shit show if you are to be queasy. Let's set the right tone for the tour. You're the man!"

Lance looked downcast, but it was only in jest. He stared at the empty cups of coffee that lay before him and pretended to wipe away a lone tear. Henry threw up his hands in the air and said, "Come on, it's not that bad! You may be addicted, but the adventures that lay ahead will drive it out of you."

Lance and his colleagues were a close-knit group, and Lance was a leader who got his hands dirty with the team. He worked hard and kept up a camaraderie with his lot. He knew the art of maintaining the dignity of his position as lead while keeping it light and friendly so as to keep his people in high spirits. His team was a jovial group who always stood by each other and never let another down. You hurt one, and the pack will rise in defense. Their bonding outran any inter-departmental politics, and Lance made sure to guard his team's interests at all times.

Finally, it was time for it all to begin. Lance looked out onto the curb and said, "The limo is here! Let's go, boys!"

Each of them picked up their luggage. Men don't have much baggage, and an attache per person was more than enough to last 7 nights. The men stood up and cheered as Lance gave Alex a high five, followed by the other two.

Together, they walked out of the coffee shop and out onto the street, gaining pace as they approached the spacious limo. They took their seats and looked at one another with eagerness in their eyes. They wondered what lay ahead of them and were excited about all that they would experience aboard The Grandiere Exaltess on their way to Canada and New England. Little did Lance know what he was in for!

Alex pulled out a bottle of Chardonnay and passed on three wine glasses, keeping the fourth for himself. He uncorked the bottle with much fête and thus set the tone for the evening. Their glasses clinked, and they all resounded, "Cheers!"

Chapter 2 – The Grandiere Exaltess

The limo arrived at the dock at about 10:30 am on a bright and sunny morning. A soft wind blew from East to West, and the four men disembarked from the limo, retrieved their luggage, and headed towards the Grandiere Exaltess. "Just look at her," said Alex in an awed whisper. She was indeed grand, standing tall and unwavering against the seas. They could hardly believe they were there. "Somebody pinch me," Henry exclaimed.

The ship was amazing. It made their nerves tingle with excitement and anticipation. They couldn't wait for the journey to begin. The sight of the ship, as well as the brine whiffs of the sea, tantalized their senses.

The majestic vessel, an epitome of maritime luxury that glides across the open seas with a commanding presence, stood before them in all its glory. Lance couldn't take his eyes off the beauty before him. Its exterior was a spectacle of modern engineering, featuring a sleek and towering superstructure adorned with numerous decks, each lined with rows of portholes and balconies that offer panoramic views of the surrounding ocean. The ship's bow, pointed and resolute, was certain to cleave through the waves with a sense of purpose, while the stern boasted expansive open decks for passengers to bask in the sun or gaze upon the receding wake.

The ship's towering funnel, bearing the insignia of the cruise line, added a distinctive touch to the skyline, expelling plumes of white smoke that blended with the azure sky. "It will be a smooth sail, from the looks of her." Theodore always had a positive outlook, and on this occasion, he wasn't just positive. He was ecstatic.

The men boarded the ship to find that its interior was a symphony of luxury, characterized by elegant atriums, winding staircases, and grand lounges. The dining areas, adorned with crystal chandeliers and fine furnishings, provided a culinary haven, while the recreational decks hosted pools, sports courts, and sunbathing areas. This floating palace of leisure and exploration was not merely a means of transport; it was an embodiment of sophistication and comfort, promising an unforgettable journey on the high seas. "I just cannot wait for our trip to begin." Lance's heightened enthusiasm was simply contagious. The others felt a thrill go up their spine. Top of Form

They found that the cruise had a variety of staterooms or cabins to suit different preferences and budgets. These ranged from interior rooms with no windows to suites with private balconies and spacious living areas.

A variety of dining options were offered, including main dining rooms, specialty restaurants, buffets, and cafes.

From casual to gourmet, the ship featured diverse menus to cater to a broad range of tastes. The thought of dining aboard this ship was more than mouth-watering. Henry was quite the foodie, and he started planning which dining areas to visit first. "The buffet would be my first preference. I always like variety. À La carte gets a little too specific, thus boring. Unless I get to taste your food too," he looked at Lance beseechingly. Lance mocked being offended and jokingly said, "I do not share food. Period."

As they moved along, they came to know that entertainment was a major highlight as the cruise ship provided theaters, live performances, musicals, comedy shows, and even casinos. Theodore was delighted. Roulette was his passion. "Will you guys give it a shot?" Lance was easygoing, but he wasn't much of a gambler. "I hope this trip does not become one big gambling session. I would be alarmed if you got home with empty pockets," he said light-heartedly.

The more they explored, the more amazed they became. Pools, hot tubs, fitness centers, sports courts, and other recreational facilities were available. They were sure to be entertained and active during the voyage.

Services on the ship included spas, beauty salons, shops, libraries, and internet cafes. Passengers were also offered laundry, room service, and medical facilities.

Lance commented that the ship must have a huge support staff to keep things going. Indeed, during their onboarding process, when they were introduced to the ones behind the scenes, it turned out that there were a host of people who ran the ship in differing capacities.

The Chief of Staff aboard the ship informed them of the diverse and dedicated team, working harmoniously to ensure a seamless and enjoyable experience for passengers.

"At the helm, officers and navigational personnel steer the ship with precision, navigating through the vast expanses of the ocean. Below decks, engineers and maintenance crews ensure the ship's systems operate flawlessly, guaranteeing safety and functionality," he said with great emphasis 'guaranteeing safety and functionality.'

"The heart of hospitality is in the hands of the ship's crew, including housekeeping staff who meticulously tend to cabins, chefs and kitchen staff who craft culinary delights, and waitstaff who provide impeccable service in dining areas. The food is to die for," he said in an attempt to keep things light.

The Chief went on to state that entertainment was curated by a team of performers, musicians, and activity coordinators, while spa therapists and fitness instructors catered to wellness needs. The ship's medical team stood ready to address any health concerns, offering peace of mind to passengers.

"Overall, the crew's professionalism, attentiveness, and expertise contribute to the vibrant tapestry of services that make a cruise voyage an unforgettable and well-supported adventure on the high seas," he finished.

Lance and his group seemed satisfied with the arrangements on board. Henry was of the suspicious kind, but his anxiety seemed to have been quelled too as he said with a reassured look, "I feel safe now."

The entire staff stood before them as they were gathered in one of the large theatres that currently held all 600 passengers and the whole crew within its vast space. The Chief began to introduce the head of each department one by one in case any passenger needed any assistance.

When the head of housekeeping, "Lexi," was introduced, Theodore, who was quite the connoisseur of women, elbowed Lance in his ribs. Lance gave him an annoyed look. "Don't start off aboard this ship, man. Have some respect."

Lexi was quite an attractive woman, with full breasts and a glowing face. Her voluptuous lips were smeared with red lipstick, which stood out against her white uniform that bore the insignia of the cruise line. Her dazzling dark brown eyes were quite a contrast to her auburn hair, but that's what made her stand out from the rest of the hospitality staff who wore the same uniform. Her slender figure was one to envy, and the way she carried herself in her pencil heels was admirable. She had a carefree air about her and glanced over the passengers. She loved her job!

Her eyes stopped briefly upon Lance, and she felt her heart flutter. After all, Lance was a handsome man, and Lexi had always found older men sexy. Their mature looks drew her in. While she had only a casual interest in Lance at this point, she turned towards her friend, Justin, and said, "Now that's some eye candy. Let's keep an eye on this one during this trip."

Coincidentally, the Chief took it upon himself to demurely remind the passengers and inadvertently the crew as well, "As is the practice of etiquette, we expect all passengers to refrain from making advances towards any of the crew members, and encourage passengers to be respectful towards everyone."

After a pause, the Chief said with elation, "So let the journey begin!"

Chapter 3 – All aboard

No sooner had the Chief finished making his announcements than Lexi dashed for the exit of the theatre. She had a lot to take care of. The passengers would soon be shown their rooms, and it was her responsibility to make sure that the housekeeping staff were on their toes.

Just as she left the theatre, Lexi turned around and attempted to catch a glimpse of Lance amidst all the chaos. The passengers were all scrambling out into the hallway, and sure enough, there was Lance giving one of his cronies a pat on the back with a merry look on his face. She turned away and hurried down the hall, still occupied with thoughts of Lance.

Lance and his colleagues made their way through the crowd and finally reached the exit into the hallway. Theodore looked around and said, "It's a mighty *big* ship." "Bigger than big daddy here?" asked Alex with a snide look at Lance. "Well, definitely bigger than your backside, young fellow," Lance quipped, careful not to go too far with his jokes yet sure to get a laugh out of the other men.

Henry took out a pack of chewing gum from his pocket and offered it to the others. Each declined, and Henry looked forlorn, "I guess we are not school boys anymore. I thought this trip could revive our youth. Nonetheless, men, too, will be men! What's say we take a go at the jacuzzi after settling in?" Lance nodded in assent.

As they reached the front desk with their luggage, they were handed the key cards to their cabins. On the other side, a stewardess called out their cabin numbers along with that of a few other passengers falling in the same sequence and asked them to follow her to their cabins.

They walked down a host of corridors. Each corridor was lined with artistic abstract paintings that were illuminated by spot lights. Soon, they reached an aisle lettered 'J,' and the stewardess walked past each cabin asking the passengers for their keys, letting them into their rooms, and leaving them on the note that they should reach out to the staff if they needed anything.

After showing three couples to their cabins, the group finally neared cabins 20 through 23. Being senior-level executives, each of them had a cabin to himself.

Alex's cabin was first in order. As the door opened, he let out a low whistle. The cabin was as luxurious as the rest of the ship. The expansive cabin, adorned with elegant furnishings, boasted a meticulously designed layout that seamlessly integrated living and sleeping areas, ensuring a sense of spacious tranquility. A private balcony invited breathtaking views of the open ocean, while large windows suffused the interior with natural light, accentuating the cabin's tasteful decor.

Premium amenities awaited within the confines of the nautical haven. The well-appointed private bathroom had a separate shower and exquisite toiletries. Technological sophistication met leisure, with a state-of-the-art entertainment system, high-speed internet, and a large flat-screen TV ensuring that passengers remained connected and entertained.

With access to private lounges and dining venues, the cabin elevated the cruise experience, offering an oasis of luxury amidst the vast expanse of the open sea.

Once they had settled in their rooms, the passengers gathered on the deck, their faces kissed by a gentle breeze. Finally, the cruise ship embarked on its journey, leaving the sheltered embrace of the shore. The atmosphere was filled with a sense of anticipation, mingled with the crisp tang of salt in the air. As they watched the shoreline gradually recede into the horizon, Lance looked out to sea. The weather, a pivotal player in this maritime overture, often dictates the initial mood of the voyage. It was a sunlit day, and the azure sky stretched endlessly, a canvas of tranquility that mirrored the calm sea below. The sun, a radiant orb, cast a shimmering dance of diamonds upon the water's surface, each cresting wave catching and reflecting the warm, golden hues.

Conversely, when the sky became overcast, the sea took on a more mysterious character. A muted palette of grays and blues dominated the scene, and the waves, though subdued, seemed to carry a certain restlessness. The ship navigated through the subtle undulations with grace, the rhythmic lullaby of the waves creating a soothing melody that lingered in the background. Occasionally, the vessel encountered playful splashes as it gently met a cresting wave, a reminder of the unpredictable temperament of the open sea.

Waves, the heartbeat of the ocean, often define the initial moments of a cruise. In calm seas, the undulating swells mimic a serene breath, cradling the ship in a rhythmic embrace. However, at that moment, with the more spirited waters, waves rose and fell with a vivacity that underscored the dynamic nature of the maritime environment. Lance felt the gentle roll of the ship, a reminder that they were navigating a living, breathing entity—the sea. As the ship ventured farther from the shore, the weather and waves intertwined to orchestrate a symphony of sensations, setting the stage for the seafaring odyssey that lay ahead.

Blown away by the beauty of the sea, the men finally decided to head back to their cabins and get easy before lunch. Lance made his way down the corridor with the other three, and before he could tap the key to open the door to his cabin, Lexi turned the corner, looking rather distracted. Lance glanced at her casually and proceeded to open the door while Lexi took in a breath. She paused in her tracks and bit her lip. "This is one handsome guy," she thought.

Lexi attempted to regain her composure quickly. "Good Afternoon, Sir," she said curtly, "Is there anything I can assist you with?" Lance liked the sound of her voice. Despite being curt, there was a tingling joviality in tone. Lance turned around and greeted her in return, adding, "Thank you very much for asking. I'm fine for now." Their eyes met for an instant. With great effort, Lexi looked away lest she made Lance uncomfortable. However, the incident did not leave a marked impact on Lance.

As Lexi walked away, she left a soft fragrance of chrysanthemums behind. Lance unconsciously inhaled deeply and was reminded of his late wife. She used to wear such floral scents. Lance was lost in thought, thinking about his youth and the romance he had shared with his wife when Theodore emerged from his cabin and nudged him. "So is that Sexy Lexi?" He snickered mischievously while Lance looked on, unperturbed. "Let's go for lunch," he said, as though nothing had transpired.

Lexi had stopped around the corner to listen in on the conversation of the men and found herself even more attracted to Lance when he had kept himself so collected in the face of his colleague's jests. He seemed like the sort of man who respected women. He had not given her any untoward looks and had held his own despite locking eyes with her. Lexi knew she was an attractive woman and was always amused when men tried to flirt with her. But what is more appealing than an upright man? That, too, a handsome man, into the bargain. Lance's perpetually cheerful look and his warm smile had set Lexi on fire, and she knew this man was more than just a crush for her.

Lexi was smart enough to have noted Lance's cabin number and went to the front desk to check the guest register. She sifted through the register until she came to cabin number 22 and nervously read his name, followed by that of the sponsoring company, "Lance Anderson, Publishers Inc."

"So the guy works in publishing, aye," she thought with a glint in her eyes. "He must be a director or at least a senior executive, looking at his age and personality." Lexi had started spinning a web of detailed descriptions regarding Lance in her mind. She was falling in love with him, and she knew it.

On every cruise trip, Lexi would mark out a favorite passenger and entertain herself with romantic thoughts about him. But this man was different. He was special. He was a man. Not just a boy.

However, the fact that making any overtures was forbidden on the ship made things difficult for Lexi. But what was life without challenges and danger? Yes, she was at the risk of losing her job, but not if she played it smartly. Besides, if Lance fell for her as strongly as she had fallen for him, then there would be little to regret. And something told her that things between her and Lance were just meant to be. Lexi sighed, "If only I could be with a man like Lance."

Lexi saw Lance a couple of times, and the maximum interaction they would have would be a nod or a respectful greeting. Lance was not one to flirt casually, and being a professional, he maintained a cordial but distant attitude. He had no interest in Lexi to begin with. But for how long?

Chapter 4 – Hidden Innuendo

The Grandiere Exaltess was afloat upon the sea, drifting further and further away from the shore. The passengers felt the ebb and flow of the tides as the ship bounced on the waves. Some experienced seasickness but soon got used to the motions of the boat.

The weather was a perfect blend of sun and shade, bringing out the beautiful sea-green color of the oft-tempestuous waters. Lance and his gang were in awe of the magnificence of the ocean. Standing upon the deck and looking out to sea, the four of them frequently felt dazed by the miracle of such tumultuous yet cadent waves.

The men spent most of their time indulging in the various activities aboard the ship, leaving their cabins in the morning only to return in the evening, absolutely spent and exhausted. Most of the passengers did the same, so the housekeeping staff got ample time to clean up the cabins in the passengers' absence.

Lexi was wont to roaming the corridors, taking care that the housekeeping staff were diligently doing their tasks and tending to the needs of the guests. She found herself ambling the aisle leading up to Lance's room more often than necessary. She felt an ache in her heart as she passed his vacant cabin, wondering what he was like as a person.

Wandering around that particular corridor gave her a strange sense of comfort. She felt closer to Lance, although this was a rather childish fancy of hers. She dreamed of being held in a strong embrace by him. The warmth of his smile when she saw him with his mates made her feel fuzzy in her heart.

The more she haunted the door to his cabin, the more she felt convinced that she was bound to encounter Lance at some point. She began to take note of his timings and hoped to be at the right spot at the right time. She had not planned what to do if she did come across him. All she knew was that she wanted to be in closer proximity to him. She imagined being close enough to feel his breath upon her skin and smell his masculine scent.

Lexi knew she may be thinking too far, but such thoughts filled her with anticipation. The idea of loving someone like Lance and being loved in return made her feel special. It seemed unrealistic, but then, an impossible dream without hope will always seem unachievable. She could always hope for love!

Lexi's crony, Justin, once caught her sauntering down the said corridor and looked at her with mock pity, his eyes twinkling humorously, "Looks like someone has fallen hopelessly in love with the old gentleman. Sweeping the floors to his door."

Lexi blushed and laughed softly before saying, "Love is an inexplicable feeling, my friend. It makes us do strange things. I'd willingly die at his doorstep if only to gain his attention. I feel drawn to him like a moth to a flame." She looked into the distance, a longing in her eyes, as loneliness weighed down her heart.

Lexi was aware that she was becoming increasingly obsessed with thoughts of Lance, desirous of a life with him. Her mind was clouded by imaginary interactions between the two of them, where they had romantic conversations all played out in her mind in intricate detail. Her attraction towards him was mysterious as she couldn't help but try to pursue him.

If things were in her hands, she would have already made the first move, but the fact of the matter was that the policies aboard the ship held her back. Restraint was difficult for her, but she had to keep herself in check for the sake of her job and to maintain some sense of decency.

She would often stand at a distance and observe Lance enjoying everything the cruise had to offer. She paid attention to the smallest of details, noting his stubble, his dressing sense, how frequently he smiled, the frankness he shared with his friends... Whenever she heard him laugh at a joke, she would appreciate his candid and unreserved nature. He made her smile to herself secretly as she hoped to share a laugh with him someday. She already felt like they shared a bond at some level and would give herself a reality check, knowing how wild her imagination was becoming.

Lance often saw her as she presumably went about her business on the ship. Beautiful women were not an anomaly in the world he came from, and they rarely had an impact on him. He was a self-assured man who kept to himself and didn't need or want attention from the fairer sex. Obviously, he had no clue that Lexi was keeping an eye on him. He was too busy having a good time to notice or sense that she was often nearby.

However, on one occasion, he had felt quite uncomfortable. He had been heaving himself out of the jacuzzi with a bare chest when he caught her gazing at him intently, a lustful look in her eyes. The moment they made eye contact, she looked away and scurried off. He thought this was a strange display on the part of a woman but did not deliberate much on the incident.

The very same day, Lance saw her walking down the corridor as he made his way to his cabin. His hair was wet, and a towel draped around his neck. He had just returned from a swim, masculinity dripping off his person.

Lexi saw him coming and continued walking in his direction. She wanted to see him up close. She knew she had no business making conversation with him, but she didn't want to miss a chance to greet him. As they both drew nearer to one another, Lexi curved her lips into a small, formal smile, "Good Afternoon, Sir. I hope you find everything pleasing on this trip?" "Good Afternoon, very well, thank you." It was nothing but a business-like interaction, but Lance had stopped to respond to her. She did not spare the chance to make the only move she could possibly make. She looked at him seductively and bit her lower lip. Words were not always necessary to express an interest in someone, and the rules for crew members said nothing about that. Lexi was always one to find loopholes!

She knew how to turn on her charm and made every effort to register her presence in Lance's mind. She wanted him to think of her as more than just the Head of Housekeeping aboard the ship. She needed him to lust after her.

She was unsure about how Lance viewed her. After all, they were a class apart, and he must have a finer taste in women. Yet she was confident that she had the power to impress Lance and make an impact. She knew she was beautiful.

Lance picked up on her advances. He felt turned on by the grace with which she had given him flirtatious looks. While she had definitely made a move, she still had some style. She wasn't cheap or unrefined, but it was obvious to him that she was by all means interested. However, he instantly regained his composure and showed no outward signs of interest. Lexi's heart longed for more.

Coincidently, Theodore had turned the corner in time to witness this interaction, and as Lexi walked away, he approached Lance, "She's coming on to you, man!" Lance rolled his eyes in disagreement.

"Theodore, could you text the others about meeting at the grand buffet scheduled in an hour? Let's put our minds on our stomachs for good measure, shall we?" Lance said, trying to change the focus of their conversation.

"Okay, bud, I'll get right on it. See you in an hour."

Chapter 5 – The Engine of Love

True to his word, Theodore had asked the rest to gather in the great foyer from where they were to proceed together to the grand buffet for dinner.

When they approached one another, they smirked at the unlikely coincidence that all four had dressed in black tuxedos. They looked dapper and felt delighted. So far, everything about this trip had been perfect, and they were having a great time. The cruise had turned out to be everything it had promised to be.

The swim had done them well and had built an appetite that only a buffet can satiate. Henry rubbed his belly and said, "Let's get going, boys." Alex, Theodore, and Lance nodded in hungry agreement.

They had been standing at the entryway of the great foyer and had to pace its entire length in order to get to the dining hall where the grand buffet was to be held.

The grand foyer was a vast expanse of gleaming marble, its reflective surface adorned with intricate patterns that shimmered under the soft glow of crystal chandeliers hanging from the lofty ceiling. The walls were decorated with large, ornate mirrors that reflected the grandeur of the space, creating an illusion of even greater spaciousness. A palette of rich, deep colors—burgundy and gold—dominated the décor, creating an atmosphere of sophistication and warmth.

At the heart of the foyer, a grand piano stood proudly on a raised platform, with a talented pianist filling the air with classical melodies and soothing tunes. The strains of music mingled with the murmur of excited conversations as passengers gathered in small groups, their eyes wide with wonder as they took in the sheer magnificence of their surroundings.

The focal point of the grand foyer was a larger-than-life sculpture of art installation, a mesmerizing glass display, and a cascading waterfall that added a touch of contemporary artistry to the classic elegance of the space.

Alex walked up to the sculpture and looked at it, commenting, "We could do with one of these at the office. Will lighten up the atmosphere."

Lance chuckled and said in an exaggerated fashion, "Why? Am I not enough?"

The group burst into laughter.

Lance pointed towards the entrance of the grand buffet and said, "Let's not be late, or we may miss the good stuff."

They strode towards the buffet, and no sooner had they entered than they were immediately enveloped in the enticing aroma of a myriad of international cuisines. The buffet was laid out on long, gleaming tables adorned with crisp white linens and elegant floral arrangements. Above, intricate chandeliers cast a warm, inviting glow, while large picture windows provided panoramic views of the endless sea, enhancing the dining experience. Alex looked around him with a startled expression, "This truly is grand."

The buffet stations were a vibrant mosaic of colors, each offering a tempting array of dishes meticulously prepared by skilled chefs. A sushi bar showcased delicate rolls and sashimi, the freshness of the seafood evident in every piece. Nearby, a carving station featured succulent roasts of beef, lamb, and ham, expertly sliced to order. The tantalizing scent of herbs and spices wafted from a grill station where skewers of seafood, meats, and vegetables sizzle over open flames.

Henry placed some sushi on his plate and looked over at Lance, "Sushi for you, Sire?" Lance smiled sarcastically but nonetheless allowed Henry to help him to some sushi.

The international flair of the buffet was evident in the diverse array of dishes. A pasta station tempted the passengers with made-to-order Italian specialties, while a stir-fry counter offered the sizzle and aroma of Asian wok cooking. The scent of freshly baked bread and pastries emanated from a bakery corner, where baskets overflowed with artisanal loaves and decadent desserts.

The dessert section was a paradise for those with a sweet tooth. Elaborate chocolate fountains cascaded velvety streams of dark and white chocolate, inviting guests to dip fresh fruits, marshmallows, and pastries. Towers of delicate pastries, cakes, and tarts beckoned with their artful presentation, while an ice cream bar featured an array of flavors and toppings for a customizable treat.

Henry rubbed his belly once again, "Remember to leave space for the best. Dessert is the heart of a buffet for me!"

Throughout the buffet, attentive and impeccably dressed staff members stood ready to assist passengers, replenishing dishes, clearing plates, and ensuring that the dining experience was seamless and enjoyable. Soft background music, played by a solo pianist, added a touch of sophistication to the atmosphere.

Lexi roamed the dining hall with an angelic air, dressed in her usual uniform but looking as graceful as ever with her hair tied back in a French twist. The music seemed to enhance her mystic touch.

She looked about the room, searching for Lance. She caught sight of him helping himself to dessert in a miserly fashion, unlike one of his cronies. Perhaps that was the secret to his well-maintained physique, she thought.

Having filled their plates, the men headed towards a table in a quiet corner of the room. On the way to their table, Lance caught sight of Lexi and impassively checked her out. She was a fine lady, but he had other things on his mind at the moment, he thought, looking down at his plate with anticipation.

Lance was really looking forward to his food when suddenly the ship quivered, and his plate flew out of his hand. It seemed that the engine had a violent jerk. Other guests were struggling with their food, and many of the women stared at the splashes of food on their clothes, aghast. There was obvious turbulence, causing the crowd to emanate squeals of fear. Even the men had lost their sense of calm as the ship tipped from side to side.

Tables shook, and chandeliers threatened to shatter. The sounds of the troubled passengers, compounded with that of moving furniture and crashing dishes, created quite a commotion. Nobody seemed to be in their element: crew members, passengers, staff, and all.

The Chief of Staff was also present at the buffet and had been seated at a table at the very front of the dining hall, an ideal place from where to address the entire crowd.

He looked bedraggled, red curry all over his front. While the turbulence had also shaken him, he gathered himself quickly and said in a commanding yet trembling tone, "Everyone, head towards the deck immediately. In case water enters the vessel, we would rather be on the deck. Worst scenario: We have lifeboats. I will go and check on what happened. Everyone on the deck, please. Don't worry. This is not The Titanic."

Lance took a quick look around the room and decided his course of action. He was a man of great resilience and nerves of steel. He knew he needed to help as many people as he could and get them onto the deck to safety. He started by addressing his mates, "Careful, there. Everyone is crowding the entrance. There is chaos everywhere. We need to remain calm. Don't push. Let me talk to this lot here.... ... Excuse me, Madam, please pass on the word that this is no time to push one another. Let's all form a queue. We will be out in no time, God Willing." Alex, Henry, and Theodore followed Lance's lead and helped all the passengers form a queue that started to move swiftly out of the entrance and head up the stairs towards the deck.

Lance and his colleagues were in the queue, climbing stair after stair at a slow but steady pace. Lexi was a few steps ahead of them, but all thoughts of Lance had been blown out of her mind by the happenings of the night. She scrambled up the stairs, praying to be delivered with safety. Suddenly, her heel snapped in half, and she tripped, crashing on the staircase with an ominous thud. Lance witnessed the scene and rushed forward, just like he would have had it been anyone else. He was not particularly bent upon helping Lexi. He reached by her side and grasped her arm firmly, pulling her off the floor. Lexi felt his strong yet gentle grip and was flustered by the heat of the moment. Lance helped brush the dust off her clothes and stood by her side, ensuring she had steadied herself. They were in close proximity.

Lexi seemed to have forgotten about their circumstances and was lost in the scent of his cologne. Lance appreciated the fact that she reached to his shoulder; so delicate and petite. He looked into her eyes, and she in his. It was as though the world had stopped spinning on its axis, and all time had frozen. Nothing seemed to matter anymore.

Lance helped Lexi onto the deck. The two of them were completely unaware of the reactions of Lance's cronies. They had witnessed the entire scene and felt the emotions shared between the two but were unable to say anything. Love is a dumbfounding sight. To see two people falling in love is akin to having witnessed the formation of the universe.

Having reached the deck, Lexi felt a bit awkward. She realized she was very near Lance and stepped back cautiously. She gazed at Lance and wondered how to react after the intimate moment they had just shared. She smiled at Lance shyly and said a hasty, "Thanks." Lance brushed it off with a shrug and pretended as though nothing had just happened between them.

Lexi reluctantly walked away as a sense of calm had been regained on the ship, given that the engine had been set right.

The Chief of Staff coughed loudly to get the attention of all the passengers and said, "There is nothing to worry about. We are on the course of our journey. This was just a minor, unforeseen setback, and we will ensure that the engine is thoroughly checked so that such an incident does not reoccur."

Feeling a bit ill at ease, they all begin to disperse. Lance found it difficult to take his mind off Lexi. Her eyes were so dazzling and innocent. She had a fresh glow on her face, and her beauty was simply ethereal. Lance was blown away like he had never been before.

Lexi was overwhelmed with emotions. Her heartbeat had increased, and she kept reliving their interaction, thinking of Lance as her savior. This kicked off the engine of love!

Chapter 6 – Clandestine Meeting at Sea

Lance had slept well despite the jolt that he had experienced at the hands of the faulty engine. He rose from his bed and quickly dressed for breakfast in a casual, half-sleeved, button-down shirt.

The men had committed to meet at 9 am in the dining hall to have a scrumptious breakfast of cereal, bacon, and eggs with other assortments of choice.

As they got together, Lance commented, "The weather is bright today. I'm glad we woke up early to get a good breakfast."

Henry seemed rather ticked off, "Need we awaken at such an ungodly hour. You forget we are on vacation."

Lance got right back at him, "We didn't board a cruise just to sleep away the time. Let's make the most of it. I certainly intend to." And Lance patted his front pocket with a sly look. His friends were not privy to his little secret.

Lance had a plan up his sleeve. Before leaving his room, he had scribbled a note and kept it in his pocket. He would wait for the opportune moment, shall it arise, and hand it over to Lexi. It was the only way of making things move forward.

The rules of the ship may dictate one thing, but Lance wasn't one to play it by the book anyway. He knew he had to take his chances. Lexi's job was at stake, but he could undoubtedly take care of that complication if it arose. Being part of the staff on a luxury cruise wasn't the only job left in the world, and Lance could very easily have her well placed elsewhere. All he wanted was for her to be his. And that wouldn't happen unless he made it happen. And so he had a plan that just needed to be put into action.

During breakfast, as the sunlight entered through the portholes that opened into the pristine dining hall, Lance looked out for Lexi and kept glancing around, much to his friends' amusement. They knew something was up with him and felt anxious to see him so distracted.

He was barely involved or interested in their conversations and seemed to be waiting for something. Theodore was seated nearest Lance and poked him in the ribs, "All good, mate? Lost somewhere?" Lance merely nodded and tried to feign an interest in their conversation, which was nothing but boring compared to his pursuit.

Lance finally caught sight of Lexi at the other end of the hall and decided to play her own game with her; if only eyes could truly talk. Lance winked at Lexi and, with a swift movement of his hand, called her to his table under the pretext of some service. His colleagues' eyes were on him, and they wondered what he was playing at. They looked at one another questioningly, wondering if Lance was really going to talk to Lexi or was this strictly professional. It was unlike Lance to act improperly, yet something seemed to have gotten into the man this morning.

Lexi blushed and wondered what Lance meant with a wink and a call to service. She was far from alarmed at his flirtations and was actually pleased to have caught his attention.

Wasn't this exactly what she had wanted? She was beside herself with emotion but had to maintain her composure lest some other crew members noticed that something was stirring between her and Lance. It was difficult for her to surmise that Lance had actually called her over to his table, and although she was teetering on the hope of something more than just a call for service, she feared disappointment and so tried to maintain a balanced head.

She walked over to his table slowly and purposefully, fixing a strand of her hair. Given that she was at the other end of the hall, there was quite a distance between Lance and Lexi. The wait seemed endless to Lance as he observed her gait and her slender figure. She had style. She had class. She had magic in every step. He was totally smitten by her. It took all his self-control not to rise from his seat and twirl Lexi across the room.

There was a simplicity about the girl that absolutely touched Lance. She carried herself well and with grace, but nothing was overdone. In his eyes, she was just perfect.

Lexi soon reached Lance's table. She stopped a few inches away from the table and stood with poise. Suddenly, she observed that Lance's friends were trying hard not to snicker. She felt a bit humiliated, and Lance glared at his companions. Lexi averted her gaze from the other men and focused on Lance.

The fact that his friends found something funny was definitely suggestive, but Lexi thought it was disrespectful for grown men to behave in such a fashion. Nonetheless, she was now aware that this was more than just a professional interaction. Why else would Lance's friends try to hide their smiles?

'Yes, Sir. How can I help you?" Lexi said in her most charming yet professional manner. She wanted Lance to see her as someone who knew her boundaries. Not someone who simply made advances and didn't know how to control herself. It was a delicate balance, and she hoped she was giving Lance the right impression. She didn't want him to think he could do her with a one-night-stand. Lance was the kind of man with whom Lexi wanted it long-term. She had to show him that she had self-respect and was not throwing herself at him. Therefore, she maintained a relatively distant attitude. Giving coy glances in the corridor was one thing, but that didn't mean he could take her for a ride.

Seeing that Lance was hesitant to speak, Lexi drew up to the table, and Lance daringly took hold of her hand, which she had lightly placed on the table before him. He felt the softness of her hand, and a ripple of pleasure passed over him. Lexi felt his touch and was taken aback by his move. His hand was firm and unshaking. He was a man who was in control.

She wondered if he had mistaken her but did not remove her hand. She was hypnotized at the moment. The others at the table wondered what was going on, but no one saw Lance discreetly slip the note into Lexi's hand.

This was his first move in the game of love. He wished he had acted sooner but had honestly not been paying much attention to Lexi at all, beautiful though she was. Lance was not a man who took an interest in women, yet Lexi had drawn him in. She was more than just the average woman. She was a goddess disguised as a human.

It had taken a while for Lance to notice her, but hopefully, the cruise would be long enough for him to make things work or at least to get the ball rolling.

Having made his move, Lance was hopeful that Lexi would respond in accordance with his desires. He not only lusted after this woman, he respected her for the grace with which she carried herself.

Lexi was surprised at Lance's move. He had been bold about it. His handsome face had been etched with what Lexi could only term as 'sincerity.' She rushed into the kitchens to read the note in peace. Justin was standing nearby and noticed the excitement on Lexi's face. He joined her as she fumbled with the note in her hand and peered at the note over her shoulder. "Oooh, a love letter?! Is this from Lance, your dream boy?" Lexi gave him an annoyed look and hid the note from his gaze, "Come now! Let's not get ahead of ourselves. We don't know what he wants yet. What are his intentions?"

Lexi unfolded the note with much pomp and show for Justin's benefit and read it aloud,

"Meet me on the deck at dawn tomorrow. The hour will cover for us with nobody on deck while the lifeboats will conceal us."

The note was short and to the point. It left many questions in Lexi's mind. Was he serious about her, or was this just a cruise romance? After all, Lexi didn't know him as a person and did not know what to expect. He may well be a player on the lookout for his next victim. Yet something in Lexi's heart told her to trust him. It may turn out to be more than just a casual affair.

Justin read the questions in Lexi's eyes and said, "Be careful, young one. You don't want to get into something that will cost you your job and leave you without man or money. Take care of yourself first. A romance is fine, but let it be on firm ground. The cruise is no place to court."

Lexi knew Justin was right. A one-off meeting on the deck may be harmless if executed with care. But she couldn't engage in romance with Lance on the cruise lest their secret gets out of the bag. That would be a big disaster.

The wee hours of the next morning found Lance and Lexi exiting their separate bedrooms with much secrecy. Each of them climbed the stairs to the deck with much apprehension and anxiety. No one was about at that early hour, and it was the perfect time to have a clandestine meeting.

Lance reached first and took up his position behind one of the lifeboats. When Lexi arrived, he let out a low whistle to indicate where he stood.

Lexi was not dressed in her uniform and looked elegant in a figure-hugging peach dress that contrasted well with the early morning hues of the sky.

Lexi joined Lance behind the lifeboat, and they both looked out at the peaceful waters. It was an amazing sight in itself, but the moment was further enhanced when two whales rose onto the surface of the water in unison. "Woah! It's a divine sign, my love. What more can indicate that God Himself wills our unison."

Lance was mesmerized by her very presence as she walked up to him. "I have been waiting for this moment with great anticipation," Lance said in a suave tone. At that opportune moment, a passing seagull left its droppings on Lexi's dress. Lexi looked disgusted. Lance used his handkerchief to wipe away the droppings. "Looks like we were not the only ones waiting for such an opportunity," he said, trying to ease the tension. Lexi smiled good-humouredly.

Lance touched her arm gently, "Tell me, O goddess, what will it take to please you? I wish nothing but to hold you in my arms."

Lexi looked into his eyes and once again saw nothing but sincerity. She didn't know what to say. It was such a sudden question. She knew she wanted to be with him with every fiber of her being. Yet she knew she must show restraint. "Let's meet at Devocion once the ship docks back in New York."

Lance suggested with hopeful approval from Lexi. "That sounds wonderful. Let's make it around 6 pm if that's okay?" Lexi added. "I will see you there, Miss Lovely," Lance said romantically with love in his eyes. Lexi smiled with intense desire.

Chapter 7 – Landing with Love

Like all things, good or bad, must come to an end, so did the trip on the cruise come to a close. A few days of joy and luxury sure had spoilt the men, but Lance, being the team lead, was determined that it would not take too much time to bring them back on track once at work.

Each of the four men was disgruntled by the very looks of it. Theodore kept searching his cabin for anything he may have forgotten. Alex was upset that his suitcase was not getting zipped up because of excess baggage, while Henry was busy separating clothes he had worn from those that were clean.

All the passengers were feeling a bit gloomy now that the trip was about to end. It felt like Sunday evening when everyone was derepressed that Monday would follow.

There was a great hullabaloo aboard the ship as everyone grappled to pack. Not only were the four of our concern, but all the passengers were gathering their clothing items, gym clothes, and swimming gear. Many had lost something or the other and were accusing the housekeeping staff of not taking care of their belongings.

There was generally an air of chaos and pandemonium, which Lexi and her staff were used to at the end of their tours, but this time around, Lexi was very excited because of the meeting with Lance that lay before her. She couldn't believe that things had moved so fast. All in one cruise, she had gone from being Lance's nobody to Lance's somebody.

Lexi focused on doing her duty. She was as poised as ever, never losing her calm as she assisted the passengers in every possible way and tried calming down those who were ferocious about having lost something. She told them that after the ship had docked, there would be a thorough clean-up of the cruise by the housekeeping staff, and any missing valuables would be duly returned. This somewhat eased the passengers who resigned themselves to utter helplessness in the face of their missing valuables.

Lance, on the other hand, was always packed and prepared. He never let his things get all hodge-podge and always made sure to keep every item he used back in his suitcase rather than leaving it lying around. That saved packing time and also kept everything neat and in order.

As everyone packed, Lance sat back and watched the entertaining show where everyone else, his cronies included, ran about in an attempt to gather their belongings. What a catastrophe! My God!

But more than being absorbed by the state of affairs before him, Lance's thoughts were occupied by those of Lexi. How could a woman be so ethereal? How could she be so divine? He was falling for her, and he was falling for her badly. He had to have her. He wanted her, not just in his thoughts and his heart. He wanted her in his arms.

There was a bounce in Lance's every step as he had something special to look forward to once the ship had docked. It was his small, little secret. Of course, he would never tell the other three for fear of being made fun of and because he was a very private person. He always projected boundaries and would never allow anyone to speak ill of Lexi. The boys were likely to think she was a one-night-stand, but Lance had more than that on his mind.

He was a lonely man with grown kids who could take care of themselves. After all, he, too, needed a companion. After his wife's death, he hadn't quite overcome the grief, but now he thought he was ready to see someone and consider the odds.

He couldn't help thinking about Lexi. Her fair complexion, her auburn hair, the way she looked that morning when they had met secretly on the deck. Everything about Lexi was mesmerizing.

The cruise neared the shore, and the gangway was lowered. Lance noticed Bill standing amidst the crowd, casually waiting for him. He waved at him and was received with a heartwarming smile. It was time to go home now, and Lance actually had reason to look forward to it.

Lexi stood at the exit of the ship, seeing off the passengers, wishing them well, and expressing her hope that they had indeed had a great time aboard the ship. When it came to doing her duty, Lexi was always a thorough professional, and Lance just loved that about her. Business is business.

As Lance left the ship, he paused for a moment and gazed into Lexi's eyes. They exchanged knowing looks, anticipation bursting in their hearts. Lexi gave him a small, curt smile but internally wished she could hug and kiss him goodbye till they met again.

A hundred words could be said just by that one look that was exchanged at the gangway. It is mysterious how one can speak through their eyes; their affair started through eye contact and had diligently grown through the same. It is such a wonder of nature.

They were to meet soon. Lance was nervous about what he would say in their first formal meeting where as Lexi was wondering about her attire. What would make her look most attractive and flattering?

Lance thought of telling her first of his late wife and his two children. After all, she must know what she is signing up for. But first, he would ease out the conversation by throwing in a few genuine compliments. He decided to take flowers for her and felt sure that she would graciously accept them.

Lexi, on the other hand, tried outfit after outfit, wondering which color would stand out against the dusky skies, for they were to meet at the small town nestling Devocion in the evening hours.

It was a small, isolated town nuzzled in a picturesque setting, surrounded by rolling hills and dense forests. The town was characterized by its sense of tranquility and simplicity, as it is far removed from the hustle and bustle of urban life. The landscape was dotted with quaint cottages and small, well-maintained gardens.

The town's architecture reflected a blend of historical charm and practicality, with buildings constructed from local materials that complement the natural beauty of the surroundings. Narrow cobblestone streets wind through the heart of the town, leading to a central square where a weathered but resilient town hall stands, echoing the town's rich history. Lance chose this locality particularly because of the isolation it offered.

The tavern itself, Devoción's, exuded an atmosphere that seamlessly blends modern sophistication with a warm, inviting ambiance. Stepping inside, patrons were greeted by an artfully designed space that reflects the brand's commitment to quality and sustainability. The interior, adorned with contemporary furnishings and accented by rustic elements, created an aesthetically pleasing and comfortable setting. Large windows allow natural light to filter in, illuminating the space and enhancing the overall airy feel.

The scent of freshly roasted coffee permeated the air, enveloping visitors in an aromatic embrace that heightens the sensory experience. Lance, being a coffee addict, inhaled the scent of coffee as though he was doing so for the first time. Muted earthy tones, complemented by vibrant greenery, contribute to a calming palette that encourages relaxation and socialization. The hum of conversation and the gentle whir of coffee grinders provide a lively backdrop, creating an environment where patrons can engage in both solitude and communal interaction.

The staff, knowledgeable and passionate about their craft, moved with purpose behind the counter, adding to the dynamic energy of the space. Whether guests were sipping on meticulously crafted espresso beverages at the sleek bar or enjoying a meal at thoughtfully arranged tables, the atmosphere at Devoción was one of refined simplicity, fostering a sense of connection to both the coffee culture and the community that surrounds this unique culinary haven.

When Lance arrived, he sat outside on the quaint bench in front, waiting for Lexi to arrive.

As Lexi approached Lance, she put her lovely manicured hands to her mouth in almost unbelief at the handsome suited sight standing up before her. "Good evening, Lexi. You look mesmerizing and beautiful!" Lance said, greeting her and handing her the flowers. "You look very handsome, and thank you, they are so pretty!" She said, reaching for the bouquet. Lance gave her a kiss on the cheek and opened the door for Lexi to enter first. Once inside, they sat in a booth in the back, secluded from the entrance.

Lance held Lexi's hands from across the table, looked into her eyes, and said, "I long to have you in my arms, sweet Lexi. You are already in my every thought with strings around my heart. I haven't had feelings like these for anyone in a very long time, if ever!"

Lexi spoke back with her head slightly tilted with admiration. "The moment I first saw you boarding the ship, I felt a jump in my heart. I think the universe has lined up a divine encounter that is making the stars sing with approval." "How beautifully said, Sweetheart!" Lance whispered to her as he leaned in for a passionate kiss. Their lips met with such affection in their minds. Just then, the server said, "Good evening, my name is Brandon. How are you this evening? Welcome to Devocion."

"Hello," they both said in unison. "Nice to meet you, Brandon," Lance said. "We will have water with lemon to start, thank you, and also a bottle of your finest white wine," Lance added.

The rest of their dining experience was magical with Lance suggesting Lexi could work with him at the office as they were in need of a receptionist in the lobby. She would brighten up the entrance to the building with her professional beauty. This would also allow them to be in a relationship with no worries. Lexi loved her job aboard the ship but had already been toying with the idea of a change in lifestyle. The thought of being with Lance made her heart practically jump out of her chest! She agreed to the proposition and said, "When may I start?" Lance smiled ear to ear as he leaned in for another sensual kiss, after which he said, "Nine a.m. Monday morning will be perfect, my Love." "Let's get out of here and go for a walk through down town for a bit," Lance suggested. They left hand in hand with the hope of continuing to get closer and getting to know more about each other through conversation as they walked.

Lance learned that Lexi's Dad was a high-school rival of his back in the day. He now secretly thinks this could be a potential dagger in his future with his newfound heartthrob. Lexi is not sure how her Dad will feel but convinces herself that he will embrace her feelings and understand. She does not know the whole story, because Lance does not share it with her just yet.

Chapter 8 – Let's Talk Marriage!

Life had suddenly become so blissful for Lance and Lexi as they met each other almost every day, given that Lexi now worked at Lance's office as a receptionist. She fulfilled her responsibilities with due diligence but was immensely distracted every time Lance passed by the reception area. It was difficult for them to keep their eyes off each other, and often, when they got off work, they would leave together. They would frequent nearby cafes or else take a walk in the nearby park. Lance felt like a teenager all over again, and Lexi was overcome by her own emotions.

In one of their initial meetings, Lance brought up the subject of his late wife and grown-up children. Lexi took the news pretty well. Given that she had come to trust Lance so much, she knew things would go smoothly. Therefore, she was very accepting of Lance's circumstances and vowed to be a friendly figure to his children. "I'll always be there for you and your children through thick and thin. May the Lord Help us." Lance was touched by her words, and he became slightly teary-eyed. He reached out to hold Lexi's hand, and they sat in silence together, absorbing the love and trust that had made them fonder of each other in a matter of just a few months' courtship.

There were days when Lance had to work late. Lexi, having fixed timings, would get off work and leave without him. Lexi longed for a day when she could be at home awaiting Lance for dinner. She hoped they could make it as far as marriage but was reluctant to bring up the topic herself as that may come off as her being too desperate. However, Lance was no fool. He could read her eyes and knew what was on her mind. And the best part was that he shared her thoughts and wanted things to move fast. He wanted to marry this woman and make her his own forever. Then, there would be no distance and just an abundance of love and togetherness.

However, the thought of facing Lexi's father loomed before them as death looms before the terminally ill. Lance had yet to tell Lexi what had transpired between him and Lexi's father, Allen. He hoped she could overlook or forgive him because he was mostly only part of the group that was bullying and not the main giver of the raz. Nonetheless, he was there and let it happen and, therefore involved. *Lexi just has to love me*, he thought—*the me who is now and not the me that was then. I have changed, grown, and learned from the past and am no longer acquainted with those browbeaters.* In fact, they had started to torment him when he tried to get them to stop the oppression. He had ventured out all on his own when he left for college, leaving that group to find their own.

Lance wondered how Lexi would feel when he told her how he had treated her father. Lance thought that maybe Lexi, too, may grow averse to him because nobody would like anybody to mistreat their father. Lance had to break it to her with great caution, choosing his words wisely.

"Lance, could you tell me what transpired between you and my dad? He doesn't want to get into it with me and says you need to explain it to me."

"Well, darling, let's walk to the bench down at the park. I will explain."

The walk felt so long, and silence loomed except for chit-chat about the squirrels and birds they saw and the beautiful weather.

They sat down on the metal bench facing each other. Lance took Lexi's hand in his and began, "My sweet, sweet Lexi. Back in high school I was in a group of football players who thought they ran the field. Your father, bless his soul, put up or had to endure razzing/bullying from us about how much smaller he was then all the other players. Whenever he would drop the ball or make a mistake, we all would say some demeaning things when we saw him out at school or in the roller rink we frequented. It wasn't so much me, but the others would really give it to him. I tried later on to get them to be different, but they started to 'out' me from the clique. I left all that young, dumb stuff in my past when I went to college. I changed and focused on my studies and knew I needed to grow up and be more like my dad: kind, caring, generous, and dedicated to a better way of life. I hope you and your father can see the "me" I have become and not hold my past against me. I regret being a part of anything having to do with someone enduring unkind acts. I am not that person in my heart."

Lexi absorbed all that Lance had spoken about the past with her Dad. She stared at their hands that were still together in front of her. The silence continued for a moment until she broke it, sincerely speaking, "Lance, I realize that was a long time ago. It was, what, over 25 years ago? You were in Junior High School, and my Dad was a senior. He should understand that maturity comes with age. No one is perfect, not even my Dad. You could talk to him and show him who you have become. I think that if you explain things to him just as you have done with me, he will see and hopefully forgive you from his heart. I still love you, Lance. I don't hold your past against you because I see who you have become: genuine, kind, and loving. "Thank you, sweetheart! That means so much to me. I want you to be my wife. We need this to be rectified with your dad so I can propose properly," Lance returned passionately. Lexi unclasped their hands and hugged Lance so hard he almost gasped. She whispered to his ear "I love you so much my sweet, gentle soulmate." Lance returned to her an "I love you too Sweetheart!"

Lance decided to take the bull by its horns and reintroduce himself to Lexi's father. However, there was an additional factor that had to be considered. Lance was quite senior in age as compared to Lexi, and that may be concerning for Lexi's father. He may want his daughter to be married to someone youthful… someone near her own age. But Lance had made up his mind. It was all worth the risk. What was the worst that could happen? Allen would object to the marriage, right? Well then, so be it. At least he had put his best foot forward. If he did not act now, he would forever regret not having given it a shot.

Lexi spoke to her father before the meeting was to take place, and her father clearly recalled Lance as the bully who had shattered his confidence, but ultimately, Lance's jeers had only served to strengthen Allen, making him the man he was today. But Allen could never forget Lance's demeaning words, taunts, and catcalls. It was etched in his mind as if it were just yesterday. It had been traumatic for him, and it had taken years for him to build himself back up and be strong enough to face bullies like Lance. It was no piece of cake. Bullying in high school has scarred many. He was lucky to have grown past it.

Nonetheless, Allen begrudgingly decided to meet Lance, just for Lexi's sake, and hoped that Lance would be able to contain himself by now and may have matured not just in years but in terms of acumen as well. Allen could go to the ends of the earth for his daughter and didn't want to see her dispirited, so he patted her on the back gently and said, "Invite the man home. I'd like to see what he has to say for himself. Not that I'm expecting much anyway. Call him over if only you believe he is indeed a gentleman."

Lance went to meet Allen, and Lexi welcomed him at her home, where her father had been waiting for his guest. Lance had brought a small gift for Allen, a pair of gold cufflinks. Allen received them, seemingly gracious, but he was sad to see Lance trying to buy his way into Allen's family. Giving away one's daughter in marriage is a tough task as it is. One wants the best for his child. How could he marry off Lexi when he knew what Lance was capable of? He feared for his daughter, and in his mind, he was quite adamant that he would never agree to this marriage. This meeting was just a formality for Lexi's sake.

Lance candidly brought up the subject of his bullying acts back in high school and apologized sincerely for hurting Allen. Allen would have none of it and said that he feared Lance would ill-treat his daughter just the way Lance had mistreated him all those years ago. An apology was not enough to appease him, and he was in no mood to hear false promises of undertaking the responsibility of his daughter's wellbeing. All he knew and cared about was that no harm should come to Lexi. Added to that were his own feelings of hurt and mistrust. How can one forget the feeling of being bullied?

Shortly into the meeting, Allen rose from his seat and left the room. He was not one to just give in to his daughter's whims and fancies and needed her to understand that he had her best interests at hand. He never wanted even the shadow of dark times to fall upon his daughter, and there was no way that he would allow the villainous Lance to be betrothed to Lexi. No, he would hear none of it! Allen, having walked out of the room, the meeting ended on a cold note, and Lance left with a heavy heart while Lexi was completely heartbroken.

She would never go against her father's will but could also never forget Lance. Such was her dilemma.

Chapter 9 – A Change of Heart

The meeting with Lexi's father had not gone well, as was pretty much expected. Burdened with a heavy heart, Lexi went to the door to see off Lance. He was completely heartbroken but had already known that it would be difficult to gain Allen's trust after all that had transpired between the two so many years ago. Allen definitely had a valid point, but he could have given Lance a chance and had Lance and Lexi unofficially engaged for a certain period of time to re-assess Lance as a person after all these years had passed. Yet, one could understand the level of his mistrust. Giving away his daughter in marriage was a delicate matter that required much deliberation.

While Lance departed from Lexi's place, he knew it was the end of it all. Lexi knew it, too. There was no point seeing each other if nothing could become of it and Lexi definitely could not go against her father's wishes. She would have to secure a new job. Seeing Lance every day would be more than she could take. Lance turned around one last time as Lexi stood at the doorway looking at Lance with tears in her eyes. As the tears rolled down her cheeks, Lance reversed his car, not knowing where he would go from there. He had lost all hope and felt as though the end of his relationship with Lexi had marked the end of the world. He didn't see the point of his life and thought that his only reason for living now was for his children.

Lexi turned around and made her way to her father's room but was unable to force herself to look into his eyes at that moment. She couldn't stop weeping silently and knew that her father would only feel tormented by his decision, yet her tears would affirm the same decision as he would think that Lance could only bring tears to his daughter's eyes.

As Lance and Lexi had stood up after Allen had left the room, Lance had taken the opportunity of Allen's absence to kiss Lexi on her forehead and say, "I will always remember you, Lexi." Lexi responded by saying, "I will always *love* you, Lance. With every breath." Lexi had walked him to the door, holding his hand gently and giving it a tight squeeze as they approached the door. Lance looked at her with love in his eyes and asked, "Can we meet one last time? I can't imagine a life without you." Lexi nodded her head fervently, holding back her tears. Lance confirmed that they would meet the next day at a local café.

Lance had said, "One last meeting will give me something to keep going. Let's meet and learn to let go. I know it is hard, but if we don't have closure, we will always hold on to one another. I know it's easier said than done, but we must go on if nothing else than for each other's sake."

Lexi agreed with him and said, "I always want you to be happy in life, and unless we move on, that will not be possible. The only trouble is that my heart will always ache for you, and I am quite sure that no matter the nature of closure we may get, nothing will put a cap on my emotions."

The next day, at the agreed time and place, Lance and Lexi met to hold hands one last time and look at each other longingly. Their relationship had been in vain, and they had come so close only to part. Life had its own way of teaching lessons, and maybe the two of them had to learn how to love and let go. Knowing that it had all ended made Lance feel bitter, while Lexi accepted her fate with a bit more grace, as it gave comfort to her heart that at least she had not displeased her father.

After sitting together for two hours or more, Lexi indicated that they had to part sometime. They could see a beautiful and romantic sunset through the glass and felt that the sun had set on their relationship, leaving them in the darkness.

As they left the café, with the intent to walk in their separate directions, Lexi touched Lance's cheek and said, "Don't miss me too much. Have hope in life and be willing to move on. I'm one to be talking as I know I can never forget you. 'Never' is only an understatement."

Lance took hold of her hand once more as they stood right outside the café and said, "You might think I am walking away from you today, but my heart will always be with you. I walk away only because our circumstances have deemed it so, or else, you know that I would never leave your side."

With a peck on Lance's cheek, Lexi turned around and began to walk away, already feeling disheartened and lonely. Her heart was filled with dread for the life that lay before her. She felt deep sadness. The only thing that tied her to life was her father.

Lance had turned his back towards her, feeling that it was altogether too much to see Lexi walking away from him. He began walking in a direction unknown to him when he heard a cry of pain and agony behind him. He instantly turned around without any expectation of what he was about to see.

The sight before him was extremely alarming. Lexi had collapsed on the grass, holding her abdomen due to immense pain and gasping for air as pang after pang of a mysterious ache raced through her body. She was overwhelmed by the sensations she was experiencing and held on to dear life, hoping to get past this. A part of her felt as though she was breathing her last. She began to lose consciousness, and as she fought to hold it together, her eyes fluttered, and the whole world appeared to be a blur. The pain was too much for her to hide.

Initially, Lance had frozen on the spot, not knowing what to do, but he quickly regained his composure and ran towards Lexi. He knew that he could manage the situation because he trusted his own collected nature. Lance was at a relative distance, and he was anxious to reach her. He couldn't run any faster. He could almost feel her pain, if not the physical pain, then at least the emotional pain and suffering she must be experiencing. There was panic in the atmosphere, but Lance had the situation under control. Just as he had managed the situation on the cruise when they had experienced turbulence, Lance was a man in his element. Almost nothing could make him lose his calm.

As Lance ran toward Lexi, he pulled out his cell phone and called for an ambulance. This was a serious medical concern, and Lexi needed to be rushed to the ER immediately. Lance hoped the ambulance would make it quickly. He knew about the nearest hospital. If only the ambulance would hurry, Lexi could be there and be given the expert care of the doctors. She needed help, and Lance was desperate to get it to her. Lance was out of breath but didn't care for himself.

Finally, Lance reached Lexi's side and took hold of her, cradling her in his arms and watching as she fluctuated between consciousness and unconsciousness. He kept assuring her that help was near and for all he cared, he would never leave her side again.

He needed her to keep breathing, for him, if not for herself. Not having much medical knowledge, Lance had no idea what condition Lexi was suffering from, but one thing was for sure: he needed her to live, and he hoped against hope that nothing would happen to his beloved Lexi. He realized the full strength of his love for her and became aware that he couldn't let anything separate them, no matter what. Especially not death.

Finally, the ambulance reached the location that Lance had precisely described. The medical team was quick to lift Lexi into the ambulance and allowed Lance to take a seat meant for the patient's attendant. The sirens blared as they swiftly moved toward the hospital and were admitted through the heavily guarded iron gates. It was not easy for Lance to see Lexi in this state as she was being driven into the hospital wearing an oxygen mask. The medical team aboard the ambulance suspected appendicitis but had left the official diagnosis to the doctors.

As suspected, the doctors quickly determined that it was indeed appendicitis, and Lexi had to undergo immediate surgery. There were no two ways about it, and the sooner they got her into the operating room, the better. Lance was asked to fill out the official paperwork. These were difficult moments for Lance. Worry and anxiety were killing him. While he was in control of the situation, he couldn't help getting overwhelmed by his emotions. He loved Lexi dearly and would not be able to bear it if anything were to happen to her.

Lance was quick to inform Allen. No matter what their personal differences were, Allen was Lexi's father and had to know of the situation. Lance dialed up Allen and spoke in clear terms, "Allen, Lexi is in the hospital undergoing surgery for appendicitis. This is no time for explanations. Please make it to the hospital as soon as you can." At first, Allen panicked but soon got his wits about him, gathered himself, making it to the hospital in the shortest time span that can be expected of a father. Not only was he concerned he was in quite a state. A father's love is exposed the most in times of such grave trouble.

Lance's concern for Lexi was etched on his face. It was clear that he loved her more than any man other than her father could ever love her. The fact that Lance was so desperate for Lexi's recovery was so obvious that only a blind man could not have seen it. Lance not only wanted but *needed* Lexi to recover. He did not seem to care about the fate of his love for Lexi anymore. He did not seem to care about what Allen thought about him and if he could ever be with Lexi. He knew he wanted her, but more that that he needed her to live.

Allen was no fool. He knew true love when he saw it, and he realized that he had never given Lance a fair chance. He had a dark history with Lance, but that didn't mean that a man cannot change as he matures. It was clear now that there was no better man for Lexi than Lance. He cared for her so much. He looked so sincere and honest in his love for Lexi that her father's heart melted, and he wanted nothing more than for the couple to be betrothed as soon as could be.

Lance was quiet and patient as they waited to hear from the doctors. He did not exchange any words with Allen, knowing that this was no time to try and make amends for the wrongs he had done towards him in the past. Allen, on his part, refrained from making conversation as he was torn between the emotions he was experiencing at the hands of his own worry for his daughter and the sight of Lance, who was tormented by extreme concern and love.

It was a matter of time before the doctor emerged, looking satisfied. He came up to Lance and Allen and sighed with relief, "The moment of danger has passed. You may see your daughter in the post-operation room soon."

No sooner had the doctor left than Allen broke down and embraced Lance with great fervor. They both cried tears of joy and walked towards the post-operation room. The pale sight of Lexi, propped on the hospital bed, brightened Lance's face as he walked toward her. Allen drew towards the bed, took Lexi's hand in his own and handed it over to Lance. This was his gesture to affirm his approval of their marriage.

The next few months included Lexi's complete healing. She became her vibrant self once again. She was so in love with Lance that she could hardly contain it all in her heart. Her Dad, Lance, and she had many visits together, becoming closer and planning the wedding. Lance's children adored Lexi and approved of her as his new wife. Their wedding day was approaching quickly. The details were finally beautifully finished, and they all were ready for the glorious day ahead.

Chapter 10 – Waters of Passion

On the decks of a grand cruise ship, where the vast expanse of the ocean stretched endlessly in every direction, a beautiful wedding unfolded like a tale spun from dreams. Here, amidst the gentle sway of the waves and the salty kiss of the sea breeze, love took center stage in a setting of unparalleled beauty and grandeur.

To celebrate his daughter's wedding, Allen had booked a cruise, and as guests stepped aboard, they were greeted by the crisp white elegance of the ship's decor, a canvas upon which the nautical theme of the wedding was masterfully painted. Rows of pristine chairs, adorned with navy blue ribbons that fluttered like sails in the wind, awaited the arrival of loved ones who had come to witness the union of the two kindred souls, Lance and Lexi. The air was filled with anticipation and excitement, mingled with the soft murmur of the ocean lapping against the hull.

At the heart of the ship, a stunning ceremony space emerged, framed by an exquisite arch laden with flowers and billowing fabric that danced in the breeze. Floral arrangements, inspired by the colors and textures of the sea, covered every corner of the ship, infusing the atmosphere with a sense of vibrant energy and natural elegance. Bouquets of roses, lilies, and orchids cascaded from every surface, their delicate petals shimmering in the soft light. Centerpieces crafted from shells and driftwood graced the tables, their intricate designs a testament to the beauty of the ocean's treasures.

Underneath a canopy of twinkling stars, the evening breeze whispered through the air, carrying with it the soft scent of the ocean. The setting sun painted the sky in hues of pink and gold, casting a warm glow over the deck of the cruise ship. As the gentle hum of conversation filled the air, a hush fell over the crowd as all eyes turned towards a solitary figure standing at the bow.

With a nervous yet determined expression, Lance stepped forward, his heart pounding in his chest as he reached into his pocket and retrieved a small velvet box. Lexi, the woman he loved, watched with bated breath, her eyes shining with anticipation and joy. With every step he took, the distance between them seemed to shrink until, at last, he stood before her, his gaze unwavering.

In a voice that trembled with emotion, he began to speak, his words a heartfelt expression of love and devotion. He told her of the moments they've shared, the memories they've made, and the dreams they've dared to dream together. He spoke of her laughter, her kindness, and the way her smile lit up his world like a beacon in the night.

And then, with a steady hand and a steady heart, he got down on one knee, the velvet box held out before him like a precious offering. The crowd held its breath as he opened the box, revealing a shimmering ring that glittered in the fading light—at that moment, time seemed to stand still as he asked the question that would change their lives forever.

"Will you marry me?"

Tears welled up in her eyes as she nodded, her voice choked with emotion as she whispered a heartfelt "yes." As he slipped the ring onto her finger, sealing their love with a promise that would endure for eternity, the cheers of their loved ones filled the air, a symphony of joy and celebration.

In that fleeting moment, surrounded by the beauty of the ocean and the love of their friends and family, two souls became one, united in a bond that is as unbreakable as it is pure. As the sun dipped below the horizon, casting its final rays of light upon the happy couple, they knew that their journey together had only just begun.

As the cruise ship glided gracefully through the sparkling waters, a sense of tranquility enveloped the deck where an intimate gathering had assembled. At the ship's bow, adorned with delicate flowers, stood a makeshift altar, where a priest awaited, a symbol of solemnity and reverence amidst the breathtaking beauty of the open sea.

Guests, dressed in their finest attire, gathered around the altar, their faces aglow with anticipation and joy. The air was alive with the gentle murmur of conversation, creating a serene backdrop for the sacred ceremony about to unfold.

As the strains of music filled the air, signaling the arrival of the bride, a hush fell over the crowd, and all eyes turned towards the aisle. With each graceful step, the bride made her way toward her beloved, her radiant smile a reflection of the love that filled her heart.

Standing side by side beneath the canopy of flowers, the couple exchanged vows that echoed across the ocean, their words a testament to the depth of their commitment and the strength of their bond. The priest, with a voice as steady as the tide, guided them through the sacred rites of marriage, his words infused with wisdom and grace.

With solemn reverence, the priest blessed the rings, symbols of eternal love and fidelity, before the couple exchanged them, sealing their vows with a tender kiss. As cheers erupted from their loved ones, the newlyweds stepped forward, hand in hand, united in heart and soul.

As the sun set in a blaze of fiery colors, casting its golden light upon the newly joined couple, the priest offered a final blessing, a prayer for a lifetime of happiness and togetherness. At that moment, amidst the vast expanse of the ocean, love reigned supreme, a beacon of hope and joy that shone brightly for all to see.

As evening gave way to night, the ship transformed into a beacon of light and warmth, beckoning guests to come together and celebrate the love that filled the air. Lanterns cast a soft, romantic glow, their flickering flames illuminating the faces of friends and family as they gathered to toast the newlyweds. Music filled the air, a joyful melody that inspired laughter and dancing as the stars twinkled overhead, casting their blessings upon the festivities.

Throughout the ship, personalized signage guided guests on a journey of discovery, leading them from one enchanting moment to the next. From the moment they stepped aboard to the final farewell, every detail was thoughtfully curated to create an experience that was as unforgettable as it was magical. Themed decor elements, such as vintage props and retro signage, evoked a sense of nostalgia and whimsy, inviting guests to immerse themselves in the romance of days gone by.

Entertainment abounded, with live music and a DJ providing a soundtrack for the evening's festivities. Guests were treated to a feast for the senses, with delectable cuisine inspired by the flavors of the sea and crafted with care by the ship's talented culinary team.

From fresh seafood to decadent desserts, every bite was a delight, a testament to the culinary mastery that elevated the celebration to new heights.

As the final moments of the night unfolded, painting the sky with hues of deep purple and soft indigo, the newlyweds found themselves standing at the very edge of the ship's deck. They shared a quiet moment amidst the gentle hum of the ocean and the distant sound of laughter and music fading into the night. With each gentle sway of the ship, they felt the weight of the day's emotions begin to settle, replaced by a profound sense of peace and contentment.

Gazing out at the endless expanse of the sea, illuminated by the moon's soft glow, they were overcome with a sense of awe and wonder at the vastness of the world before them. At that moment, they realized that their journey together had only just begun – a voyage filled with endless possibilities, shared dreams, and boundless love.

Surrounded by the timeless beauty of the ocean, with its ever-changing currents and infinite depths, they felt a sense of connection to something greater than themselves. It was as if the waves whispered secrets of love and life, carrying with them the promise of adventure and discovery that lay ahead.

With hearts full of gratitude for the love they shared and the blessings that surrounded them, they made a silent vow to cherish each moment, to weather life's storms together, and to celebrate every triumph and joy that came their way, for they knew that no matter where their journey took them, their love would remain steadfast and true – as boundless and infinite as the sea itself.

As the ship slowly disappeared into the horizon, carrying them towards their happily ever after, they held onto the magic of the moment – a precious memory that would be etched into their hearts for years to come. For in that fleeting instant, amidst the beauty of the ocean and the promise of a new dawn, they knew that they were exactly where they were meant to be – together, forever and always.

Made in the USA
Middletown, DE
22 August 2024

59019141R00080